You'll find pictures of suspects, notes, and even puzzles! If you can solve them, then you'll know you're on the right track to figuring out who's behind the mystery of the Devilish Donut! So sharpen your pencil, get out your magnifying glass, and turn the page for your first Case Files entry!

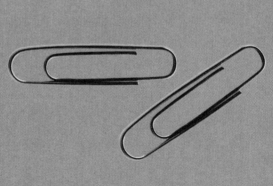

From the desk of
Mystery, Inc.

"SNRKL MRCH CHMPCHMP SNRKL GULP AHHHHH!"

The unmistakable sound of Shaggy and Scooby's eating filled the Mystery Machine as the van cruised down the empty city streets.

"Save some for the rest of us, Shaggy!" Fred called back.

"Yeah, we like donuts too, you know," Daphne added.

Shaggy and Scooby-Doo looked at each other guiltily. Patches of white powdered sugar coated their lips.

BUUUURRRRPPPP! Scooby's belch very nearly blew the roof right off the van.

"Rexcuse ree," he said, holding his paw over his mouth.

"I think what Scoob meant to say was, like, 'too late,'" Shaggy said.

Daphne and I both turned around — we were totally surprised.

"You mean to say that you two just ate an entire box of donuts all by yourselves?" I asked, shocked. Even for Scooby and Shaggy, that was a lot of donuts!

Hi. I'm Velma Dinkley, and this is Daphne, Fred, and of course Shaggy and Scooby. We're the gang from Mystery, Inc. and we're really glad you could join us in the Mystery Machine. We've just come back from a super-tough case — so tough that we haven't even cracked it yet! We thought we'd take a little break to look over our case files — we were hoping you might be able to help us analyze them!

Shaggy shrugged as Scooby slid the empty box behind his back.

"What donuts?" Shaggy asked innocently.

Daphne and I continued to stare at them. I guess it worked, because Shaggy and Scooby looked really guilty!

"We're sorry, Daph," he said. "Sorry, Velma. Sorry, Fred. It's just that when we got a whiff of those fresh-baked treats, we couldn't control ourselves. If you think about it, it's, like, really the donuts' fault for being so delicious and yummy-smelling."

Fred parked the van at a meter on the street. "This looks like the place," he said.

"And not a moment too soon," I added.

We had just gotten a call from a friend of Daphne's uncle, named Metal Man McGillicuddy. Someone had been sending him threatening phone calls and notes. He sounded really freaked out, so we hurried right over to his place.

Shaggy and Scooby jumped out of the van and onto the sidewalk. We all followed them. The streets were pretty empty, since it was so early on a weekend.

"So, like, what's the deal?" Shaggy asked.

Entry #1

"Where are we going?"

"Just a few doors down on the right," Daphne said.

Shaggy looked up and saw a big red and black sign hanging over his head. "AAAHHH!" he screamed. Startled, Scooby jumped into his arms.

"Like, this place is our worst nightmare, right, Scoob?"

"Ruh-huh." Scooby nodded vigorously in agreement.

"Come on, it's no big deal," coaxed Daphne.

Personally I didn't see what the big deal was either. If you solve the puzzle on the next page, it will tell you where we were going. Then maybe you can figure out why Shaggy and Scooby were so freaked!

Puzzle #1

Jinkies! Scooby and Shaggy's favorite words have been hidden!

See if you can find them all, then unscramble the leftover letters to find out where this mystery takes place — and why Shaggy and Scooby are upset!

Donuts **Pizza** **Soda**
Ice Cream **Hamburgers** **Sundae**
Hot Dog **Lasagna** **Scooby Snacks**
Danish **Potato chips**

the muscle factory: _ _ y _

s	❋	❋	f	❋	❋	h	❋	m	❋	❋
k	p	❋	❋	i	h	r	❋	s	t	❋
c	a	i	a	c	❋	o	o	❋	❋	❋
a	❋	h	h	e	❋	d	t	❋	❋	❋
n	❋	s	e	c	a	❋	❋	d	s	❋
s	❋	i	l	r	o	d	o	o	o	c
y	❋	n	❋	e	❋	t	n	n	❋	g
b	l	a	s	a	g	n	a	u	❋	❋
o	❋	d	❋	m	❋	❋	❋	t	s	❋
o	❋	y	❋	❋	❋	c	❋	s	o	❋
c	❋	g	❋	❋	m	a	z	z	i	p
s	r	e	g	r	u	b	m	a	h	❋

Super! You solved your first puzzle, so now you know where the mystery takes place. Now let's take a look at what happened when we went inside the Muscle Factory.

From the desk of
Mystery, Inc.

We walked into the reception area and were met by a man whose muscles bulged under his tight shirt.

"I'm Metal Man McGillicuddy, and welcome to my Muscle Factory," the man said. "I really appreciate you kids coming to take a look at my place."

STAY AWAY FROM METAL MAN'S ~~MUSCLE~~ FLAB FACTORY!!!

Metal Man

"Well, you sounded so upset we wanted to come over as soon as we could," said Daphne.

"What exactly has been going on?" I asked Metal Man.

"Someone wants me to shut down the Muscle Factory!" Metal Man exclaimed.

"What do you mean?" Fred asked.

"Well, I found this on the front door a few days ago." Metal Man handed Fred a piece of paper.

"And there are plenty more like it all around the neighborhood!" Metal Man continued. "My business is at an all-time low! And to top it off, I've been getting threatening phone calls. Today, a voice on the phone told me to close the Muscle Factory . . . or else!"

"Yikes!" exclaimed Daphne. "It's a good thing you called us. We'll find out who's behind all this."

"Yeah," added Fred, "Mystery, Inc. is on the case!"

Just then a woman wearing a Muscle Factory T-shirt and black workout pants came into the gym. She carried a black and red Muscle Factory gym bag. Her red hair was pulled back into a severe ponytail.

"Morning, Gayle," Metal Man said. "These are the kids I told you about. Kids, this is Gayle Storm, our top personal trainer."

"You look very familiar," Daphne said. "Have we ever met before?"

Gayle Storm

"Nah, I get that a lot," Gayle said as she walked over to a bench and put her left leg on it. Then she rested her left arm on her left leg and bent over slightly. She raised and lowered an imaginary dumbbell.

"This is why you recognize me," Gayle said, flexing her arms with each motion.

"Jinkies! Now I know! I've seen you all over the city!" I said.

Metal Man nodded and explained that Gayle Storm had been in all of his billboard and magazine ads since he opened the gym five years ago. Gayle tried to look modest, but she was obviously pleased to be the centerpiece of the gym's advertising.

"I've got all of the old brochures sealed and framed on my wall at home," Gayle admitted. "I'm building an archive to pass along to future generations of personal trainers so they may be inspired by my example. You know, I've even developed my own exercise techniques."

Metal Man nodded and said, "Show 'em the roller weights, Gayle."

Gayle unzipped a gym bag and lifted out a pair of in-line skates. They looked like normal in-line skates, except for the size of the wheels.

Metal Man's ↑
brochure

"Jeepers, those are the biggest wheels I've ever seen," Daphne said.

Gayle nodded. "They should be," she said. "Each wheel weighs nineteen ounces. These four wheels add four-point-seven-five pounds to the skate, making for an excellent work-out for the legs."

"Oh, my!" gasped Shaggy.

"Who uses those things?" asked Fred.

"So far, I'm trying them out on one client," Gayle said. "I've still got some kinks to work out."

Gayle packed up her gym bag and whisked it off the ground like it was nothing more than an empty pocketbook. As she passed the front counter, something on it caught her eye. Gayle stopped dead in her tracks.

"Myron! What is this?" she shouted.

"Like, who's Myron?" Shaggy asked.

"I am," Metal Man said with a sigh. "Gayle's the only person around here who still calls me that, but only when she's mad at me."

Gayle picked up a brochure from the counter and held it out for all to see. "What's wrong with this picture?" she asked.

"You mean besides the fact that you're not in it?" Metal Man asked. He seemed to be expecting the question.

"This is a travesty! It's unheard of! How could you have a Metal Man's Muscle Factory brochure without me?" Gayle demanded.

"It was time for a change," Metal Man replied. "Don't take it personally, Gayle. You're still the best trainer we have, and nothing will ever change that."

"But what about my archive? How will I be able to be a model for future generations of personal trainers if they don't know I exist?" Gayle asked with desperation creeping into her voice. "Ahhh, forget it! Thanks for ruining my day and my life, Myron!"

Gayle stormed into the women's locker room and slammed the door so hard it rattled the pictures on the lobby walls.

"Gosh, Metal Man, she seemed mad!" said Daphne.

"Oh, don't worry about her," said Metal Man. "But since you kids might be here for a while, why don't I give you a little hands-on tour of my gym. "There's plenty of extra workout gear in the locker rooms for you to change into."

We all thought that was a neat idea — except for Shaggy and Scooby of course.

"Um, like, I think I left my sneakers in the Mystery Machine — I'll just be right

Hans ↗

↖ Franz

back," Shaggy said.

"Reah, ree roo!" Scooby added.

"Not so fast, boys. Hans! Franz!" Metal Man cupped his hands to his mouth and yelled into the gym. Suddenly two huge muscle-bound men appeared. They took one look at Shaggy and Scooby and hoisted them into the air like Shaggy and Scooby were giant barbells.

"Little puny man," one of the muscle men said to Shaggy.

"It's time to pump you up," said the other.

"Zoinks!" Shaggy cried.

"Ruh-roh!" Scooby barked.

"Like, I never thought I'd say this, but don't we have a mystery to solve?" Shaggy pleaded, wriggling in the air.

We all had to laugh at Shaggy and Scooby — it looked like we found the one thing that scared them more than mysteries — exercise!

"Ahhh-hem," Shaggy said loudly. "Does this elevator also go, like, down?"

"Hans, Franz," Metal Man nodded to the two muscle men, who suddenly dropped Shaggy and Scooby-Doo to the ground in a heap.

"Hey, man, like, what's with those muscle-bound creeps!" exclaimed Shaggy.

"Hans and Franz are harmless," replied Metal Man.

Hans and Franz gave Shaggy a dirty look as they skulked off.

"Like, they don't look harmless to me!" Shaggy muttered.

"C'mon, gang, let's go get changed," Fred said as he led the way into the gym.

I think we may have met someone worth remembering. Before we go any further, solve the puzzle on the next page to find out the name of our first possible suspect.

Entry #

Puzzle #2

This crossword puzzle is sure to give your brain a workout! When you're done with the puzzle, unscramble the letters in the green shaded boxes to find out who the first suspect is!

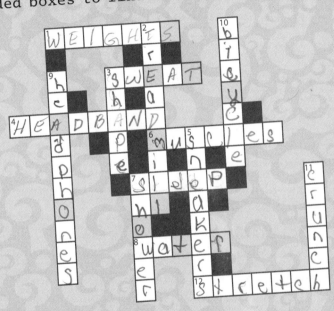

ACROSS
1. THIS IS WHAT YOU LIFT TO MAKE MUSCLES
3. WHEN YOU HAVE A HARD WORKOUT YOU ____
4. WEAR THIS TO KEEP YOUR HAIR OUT OF YOUR EYES
6. WEIGHT LIFTERS HAVE BIG ____
7. TO STAY HEALTHY, IT'S IMPORTANT TO EXERCISE AND GET LOTS OF ____
8. DRINK THIS WHEN YOU GET DEHYDRATED
12. WHAT YOU CAN DO TO A RUBBER BAND, AND TO YOUR MUSCLES BEFORE A WORKOUT

DOWN
2. YOU CAN RUN FOR MILES ON THIS, BUT NEVER GET ANWHERE
3. TO BE IN GOOD ____ MEANS TO BE HEALTHY
5. WEAR THESE ON YOUR FEET FOR RUNNING
7. TAKE ONE OF THESE AFTER YOUR WORKOUT AND YOU WON'T BE STINKY
9. WHEN YOU PUT THESE ON, YOU CAN LISTEN TO MUSIC AND NO ONE ELSE CAN HEAR
10. THIS HAS TWO WHEELS AND PEDALS
11. A FASTER SIT-UP

The first suspect is: _ _ _ _ _ STORM

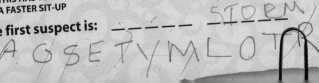

AGSETYMLOTR

Figuring out that puzzle really gave your problem-solving skills a good workout, huh? So now you know that we're keeping an eye on Gayle.

From the desk of
Mystery, Inc.

We were about to follow <u>Metal</u> Man through the doors of the reception area and into the main gym when a skinny man scampered out of the men's locker room.

"Metal Man McGillicuddy!" the man shouted. "I've got a bone to pick with you!" Upon hearing the word "bone," Scooby's ears perked up, and his tail started wagging.

"Rone? Rone?" he asked, looking around.

"There's no bone, Scooby," I said. "It's just a figure of speech. It means someone is upset about something."

"Maybe that skinny guy is upset about how badly his T-shirt fits," Shaggy said.

Everyone noticed that the man's Muscle Factory workout shirt hung off his body.

He was so scrawny that the blue backpack he was wearing made him hunch over.

"I want my money back!" the man announced.

"Take it easy, Mr. Viney," Metal Man said. "What's the problem?"

Mr. Viney's eyes nearly popped out of his head in anger.

"What's the problem? What's the problem?" he cried. "Just look at me! I'm the problem!"

We all studied Mr. Viney's spindly frame.

"Excuse me, sir, but exactly what's wrong with you?" asked Daphne.

Metal Man shook his head. "I think I know," he said. He stepped behind the counter at the front desk. After a few mouse clicks and keystrokes, the printer alongside the computer whirred to life. It spat out a picture that Metal Man grabbed from the tray. We huddled around the photo. It was a picture of the same man who stood in the lobby, fuming. At the bottom of the photo, the words "Jackson Viney, Day 1" were written.

"Hey, nice picture, dude," Shaggy said.

"It's not a nice picture!" Jackson Viney barked. "It's me, six weeks and one day ago today, but it may as well be a picture you took yesterday. Where are my muscles? I want my muscles! You promised me muscles in six weeks!"

At that point, Mr. Viney pulled this folded-up brochure from his pocket and waved it in front of Metal Man's face.

Metal Man carefully took the brochure, opened it up, and scanned the contents with his eyes.

"There's nothing in here about a six-week guarantee," Metal Man said. "All it says is that if you follow our program, you can begin to notice a difference in six weeks. Did you follow our program?"

"Of course!" Mr. Viney replied.

Metal Man folded his arms and raised one of his eyebrows in disbelief. Mr. Viney rolled his eyes and sighed.

"Oh, all right," he admitted. "I didn't use Gayle's stupid roller weights." Jackson Viney let the blue backpack drop to the ground. It landed with a loud *SPLOCK!* "But that's not the point!" he bellowed in a very squeaky voice. "I haven't gained an ounce of muscle, so I want my money back or there's going to be trouble with a capital T!"

If you follow my program in just six weeks you can begin to notice a difference!

Steve — boy he sure looks mad!

YEOW!

Jackson Viney's complaints were suddenly interrupted by a loud shriek.

"You haven't heard the last of me," Jackson said as he shuffled out the front door.

Just then an athletic-looking man came running into the reception area where we were standing. The man was waving a small dumbbell.

"Metal Man, your two-bit dumbbell nearly cost me a broken toe!" the man said.

"Whoa, calm down Steve. What happened this

time?" Metal Man asked.

"I put the dumbbell down to tie my shoe, and it rolled over my foot!" Steve replied.

"Steve, how many times do I have to tell you, if you don't handle the equipment properly, you're going to get hurt!" Metal Man sighed, fed up.

"Excuse us, Metal Man, we're going to go and get changed now," Fred said. We were all glad to have a reason to leave the awkward situation.

"You go right ahead, kids, I'll see you in the main gym in a few minutes." With that, Metal Man went back to arguing with Steve, and we headed toward the locker rooms.

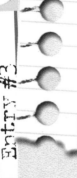

Poor Metal Man! There sure were a lot of angry people in his gym! But there was only one person who really stood out to us. Can you guess who it was? The answer to the puzzle on the next page will let you know for certain. Good luck!

Puzzle #3

This sure is one weird list! Can you make sense of it?

Follow these instructions:

1. **Cross out all the breakfast foods.**
2. **Cross out all of the "b" words.**
3. **Cross out the numbers.**
4. **Cross out the things that people read.**

fourteen buffalo angry Nine Grits omelets
muscles Granola is fruit Eighty-nine comics
twelve Textbook they toast bagel nine
Blue and ten magazine Oatmeal bananas
yogurt Blacksmith more Palms eighty-Six
Eggs one Jackson baby Seventy-seven
newspaper Cereal novel Forty-eight Basket
Blueberry wants danish thirty-five signs

Rearrange the words that are left to make a sentence below. It will tell you who the suspect is and their motive!

_____ Viny _____ Jackson is _____ angry

_____ and _____ wants _____ more muscles !

So, how'd you do? If you solved that puzzle correctly, you'll know that Jackson Viney really caught our attention. So now we've already met two possible suspects, and we haven't even made it into the gym yet! Keep reading to see what happens when we go all the way into the heart of Metal Man's Muscle Factory.

From the desk of **Mystery, Inc.**

We changed into our Muscle Factory workout clothes in the locker rooms and met up in the main gym.

"Jeepers, look at all this equipment!" Daphne gasped.

The main gym was an enormous open area that looked as big as a football field. Small groups of exercise equipment were clustered together. There were treadmills, stationary bicycles, and elliptical trainers. There were more weight machines than you could count. In one area, I noticed jump ropes and large exercise balls. Another area held a vast assortment of free weights. One wall

Metal Man napped these pictures of us.

Pretty sporty, huh?

was mirrored from end to end.

"Jinkies, there's even more up there!" I said, pointing up. A running track on the second level encircled the entire room. Glass walls lined one side of the track. Behind the glass walls were three aerobics workout rooms. A cargo net for climbing practice hung down from one side of the track.

The Muscle Factory

"This is one serious exercise club," Fred said.

"But there's more to fitness than just exercise," a woman said from behind us. We turned around and met a young woman with blond hair and a blue track suit. She was holding a picnic basket on her right arm. Shaggy and Scooby's eyes locked on to it as their mouths began to water.

Polly Fiberfeld

"Proper physical fitness is the result of exercise and a healthy diet," the woman said. "And that's where I come in. I'm Polly Fiberfeld, and I've created a new line of food products aimed at helping your body thrive."

The woman reached into her picnic basket. Shaggy's eyes widened in anticipation.

"Man, I hope she's got a pizza in there, Scoob," he whispered.

She pulled out two small nutrition bars wrapped in red and silver foil. She held up the bars as she began to speak.

"These are . . ." she began, but before she could finish her sentence, Shaggy and Scooby grabbed the bars and ate them whole, wrapper and all.

"Shaggy!" Daphne scolded.

"BUUUURRRRRRP!" Shaggy belched.

"Sorry about that," Fred said to Polly Fiberfeld.

Even though she was still a little shaken by Shaggy and Scooby's lightning-quick assault on the nutrition bars, Polly smiled.

"That's, uh, okay," she said. She looked directly at Shaggy and Scooby and asked, "Well, what do you think? They're not too

FIBERFELD'S FIBER TREAT

heavy, are they? My last batch were like bricks."

Shaggy thought for a moment. "Tastes kind of like . . . " he began.

"Ree rark," Scooby chimed in.

"No, not tree bark," Shaggy said, rubbing his chin. "More like . . . "

"Randpaper?" offered Scooby.

Shaggy shook his head and said, "Nope . . . I'd say more like Styrofoam peanuts and acorn shells. And tin foil."

Polly was surprised at Shaggy's and Scooby's assessments of her nutrition bar. She turned to us.

"And why exactly would they know what tree bark, sandpaper, and Styrofoam peanuts taste like?" she asked.

"Yeah, you don't want to go there," Daphne confided.

Polly nodded in understanding. "Well,

thank you for your honest opinion," she said.

"You're welcome," Shaggy said. "Can Scoob and I have, like, seconds?"

Scooby rubbed his stomach and nodded his head eagerly.

"Sorry," Polly said, looking over our shoulders. "Metal Man is on his way, and he doesn't like me giving out food. He's got his muscle goons keeping an eye on things." She tilted her head toward the back corner of the gym. There stood Hans and Franz, the two muscle men who had picked up Shaggy and Scooby.

"I've had to sneak my nutrition bars to Jackson Viney," Polly continued. "All I want to do is help people eat healthfully, but Metal Man doesn't seem to see things my way. Ooo — gotta run!"

Polly took off and disappeared through one of the doors along the mirrored wall just as Metal Man came over to us.

"Who were you talking to?" he asked.

"Someone named Polly Fiberfeld," Fred answered.

Metal Man shook his head. "I've asked her several times to stop using my members as her guinea pigs," he said. "I know she means well, but I don't want to get into the food business. This place is just about exercise. And speaking of exercise, what do you say, fellas?"

"Like, how about, 'See ya later,'" Shaggy grinned.

"Very funny," Metal Man said. "All joking aside, boys, when we're done here, you're going to thank me. Now let's get cracking!"

Shaggy paled. "I, like, hope he doesn't mean our bones," he moaned.

I think we may have met our third suspect. Figure out the puzzle on the next page to find out who it is!

Check out the pairs of words on the opposite page. Do you see anything interesting about them? Each pair of words is almost exactly the same—except for one important letter!

Puzzle #4

Find the letters that are different in each pair then place them in the spaces below to spell out the name of our third suspect.

We've done the first one already to get you started.

GRIN and REIGN
DREAD and LADDER
PEARS and PRAISE
RANGED and GROANED
STRAW and WASTER
YACHT and CHAT
LEAPS and SALE
BRACES and CARES
DIARY and FRIDAY
LIPS and SPILL
STARED and DATES
CLEAR and CRADLE
RIPPLE and FLIPPER
NOTES and STOLEN

Entry #5

So now we know that Polly Fiberfeld is our third suspect. She's mad that Metal Man won't le her give out her nutrition bars at the gym. Now it's more important than ever for you to keep you eyes open. After all, you never know what's goin to happen next!

From the desk of
Mystery, Inc.

"Warming up properly is about the most important thing you can do before a workout," Metal Man said as he led us over to the exercise bicycles. "Shaggy, Scooby, why don't you two start on these for a few minutes."

Shaggy and Scooby shrugged and climbed on two bicycles. They began pedaling.

"Hey, this isn't too bad," Shaggy said. He folded his arms behind his head, closed his eyes, and leaned as far back as he could, all while pedaling. Scooby-Doo did the same. Suddenly, Shaggy noticed a familiar fragrance wafting through the air.

"Hey, Scoob, do you smell that?" he asked.

Scooby and Shaggy gettin' physical

Scooby lifted his head and snuffled an enormous whiff. His eyes lit up. "Reah," he said. "Ronuts!"

"That's what I thought!" Shaggy cheered. He opened his eyes and saw a tiny chocolate-covered mini-donut rolling past the bicycles. Another one soon followed, then another, and another, and another.

"It's, like, the march of the donuts!" Shaggy cried. "C'mon, Scoob, let's join the parade! Scooby?" There was no answer — Scooby had already begun to follow the trail of donuts.

"Wait for me, Scooby-Doo!" Shaggy called as

he jumped off his bicycle. Just as Shaggy's feet touched the ground, one of the donuts rammed into his foot.

"YYYEEEEEEOOOWWWW!" Shaggy cried, hopping up and down. "That's, like, the heaviest donut I've ever felt!" He grabbed his foot and heard Scooby yelp in pain. Pretty soon, the gym was filled with people yelping and yeowing in pain as the little donuts rolled over toes, banged into shins, and knocked into exercise equipment.

Metal Man, Fred, Daphne, and I ran over to see what was going on.

"What's going on in here?" Metal Man wondered. But before he could answer, a giant donut waddled into the gym! Except for the fact that it had two stubbly little legs and eyes that glowed devilishly, it looked like a real donut, complete with frosting and sprinkles! Its disembodied voice filled the gym.

"RAHAHAHAHA!" the voice cackled. "Donuts, donuts everywhere but not a treat to eat!"

"Get out of my gym!" Metal Man ordered. The giant donut stood firm.

"Why so grumps, gramps?" asked the voice. "Blood sugar too low? How about a dozen donuts?"

With that, the giant donut sent forth a barrage of little donuts that pelted Metal Man's legs.

"Ouch! OOCH! Cut it out!" Metal Man cried, jumping around to keep the little donuts away. But the little donuts seemed to have minds of their own and kept rolling and bumping into Metal Man's legs. One jumped up and hit him behind the right knee, buckling his leg and sending Metal Man down to the floor. The tiny donuts set upon Metal Man so fiercely that he couldn't even defend himself!

"Bring him!" the Devilish Donut commanded. The little donuts rolled themselves into a circle around Metal Man. Then two by two, they rolled themselves under his back. Before he knew it, Metal Man was being rolled away by the army of little donuts. We tried to rescue Metal Man, but the Devilish Donut blocked our way.

"Let this be a warning to all you health-obsessed freaks," the donut warned. "Metal Man's Muscle Factory is now the Donut of Doom's Flab Factory! And anyone who tries to exercise will meet the same fate as Metal Man. You have been warned! RAHAHAHAHAHA!"

The giant donut monster rolled itself down the hallway toward the locker rooms. The remaining mini-donuts slammed themselves into three of the bicycles, knocking them over. The mini-donuts scrambled together and rolled after the master donut. The other folks in the gym ran out as Fred made a diving catch to grab one of the minis. He was too slow and came up empty-handed.

Before anything else happened, I took a picture of the crime scene, which you'll find on this page. Examine it. Do you notice anything suspicious that might be a clue? Solve the puzzle on the next page to see if your guess is correct.

(handwritten) Tiurnfimtata

Puzzle #5

Finish filling in the grid with the letters below. The letters are in the column that they belong in, but not the correct row. When you're done, read the message and follow the instructions to discover the first clue.

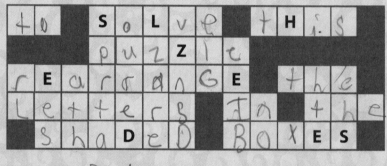

Grid (handwritten answers):

t	o		S	o	L	v	e		t	H	i	s
			p	u	z	z	l	e				
r	E	a	r	r	a	n	G	E		t	h	e
L	e	t	t	e	r	s		J	n		t	h	e
	s	h	a	D	e	D		B	o	X	E	S

Letters below:

```
    A E Z
 O    U E S              T E
R S T R R   V G B O    H S
T E H P O R N L I N T
L  A T   A D E E T X I H E
```

_n_ _u_ _t_ _r_ _i_ _t_ _i_ _o_ _n_ _b_ _a_ _r_

It was Scooby who spotted the nutrition bar first! Looks like the Devilish Donut was hungry! But before we look around the gym for more clues, I'm going to let Shaggy take over the case files notebook for a bit. Hope you enjoy his observations

Finally! Like, Scoob and I have been waiting for a chance to put in our two cents!

Since the gym (Yikes! Like, the very word makes me shudder!) is so huge, Fred thought we should split up to cover more ground. Now, me and Scoob like splits, as long as there's a banana involved! Somehow I didn't think that was what Fred had in mind. Man, was I ever right!

So back to splitting up. Daphne and Fred went to check out the locker rooms, and Velma was going to the reception area to see if there was any info on the computer. That left me and Scoob to our own devices. I could see a stack of mats with our names on them — perfect for a power nap. But, like, Velma had something else in store for us.

"Shaggy and Scooby. I want you to comb the exercise floor," she said.

"Should I, like, brush and style it, too?" I asked. Man, sometimes I crack myself up.

"Very funny, Shaggy, but I want you and Scooby to see if you can find anything around the treadmills, exercise bikes, and other equipment in this area," she told us. "It's small enough to keep you out of trouble . . . I hope."

"Don't worry about a thing, Velma," I said, "Scoob and I have everything under control." Little did Velma know, I had my fingers crossed behind my back! But still, Scooby and I got down to business.

Scooby looked low while I searched high. Scooby sniffed around all the stationary bicycles and treadmills. I explored the

Scooby-Doo sniffin' for clues

equipment — there were lots of jump ropes and exercise balls.

"Find anything, Scoob?" I asked.

"Ruh-uh," Scooby replied, sniffing along the floor.

Whoa, what's this! I came upon two short posts about six feet apart. The ends of a jump rope were attached to the tops of the posts. There was a remote control in a holster attached to the left post.

"Put 'em up, partner," I said to Scooby as I grabbed the remote and pushed a green button. Suddenly there were three short *BEEPS* followed by a loud *BRAAAAP*. Man, Scoob nearly lost it. Slowly the jump rope attached to the posts started turning on its own. Now, this I had to try. I jumped in and started skipping.

"Hey, Scooby-Doo, check this out," I called.

"Raunted rump rope?" Scooby asked. We've had some pretty bad experiences with things that move on their own, so I didn't blame Scoob for being nervous.

"No, good buddy," I reassured him, "It's, like, an automatic jump rope!"

"Rait for ree!" he barked. Scooby hopped in and began jumping alongside me.

"I wonder what these other buttons do," I said, still holding the remote. I pushed an orange button, and the rope began turning faster.

"Ruh-oh!" Scooby cried, his doggie legs working double-time.

"I know wh-wh-wh-what you m-m-m-m-mean," I said — like, I could barely keep up! I pushed a yellow button on the remote, and the jump rope suddenly started going the other way.

"Tails up, Scoob!" I called. "It's coming from behind now!"

Scooby and I watched our reflections in the mirror — that helped us keep up with the crazy jump rope contraption! Suddenly I pushed the red button on the remote, and the rope stopped short, sending me and Scooby tumbling to the floor. Just a warning — this next part is pretty creepy — you may not want to read it if you're scared of giant baked goods!

"RAHAHAHAHAHAH!"

Like, suddenly a terrible cackle came from behind me and Scoob. Man, I should have just covered my eyes, but instead I looked in the mirror in front of me. That's when I saw an overgrown pastry running toward me!

Grrr!

"Like, run, Scoob!" I yelled. "It's the Devilish Donut!"

"I warned you about doing exercise!" the donut hollered. "Now someone else will pay!"

We dove behind a knocked-over treadmill and watched as the Devilish Donut let out his army of mini-donuts! They went rolling across the gym floor.

Suddenly Daphne came running into the gym. "What's going on?" she asked. "I heard some kind of commotion out here."

The mini-donuts changed direction

and headed for Daphne. They scooped her up and rolled her away through a set of mirrored doors, and the big creepy cruller followed.

"That's two!" the evil donut crowed. "Only ten more for a perfect dozen! RAHAHAHAHAHAHA!"

YOINKS! Like, Daphne's been kidnapped! We heard her cry out for help, but her voice faded away. I checked to see that the coast was clear before Scooby and I came out from our hiding place.

Just then Fred and Velma raced into the gym.

"What happened?" asked Fred.

"Those little donut creatures took Daphne!" I told him. "Man, that does it, I'm swearing off those mini-donuts forever!"

"Ree roo!" Scooby agreed.

"Take a look at this," Fred called. "Looks like one of those mini-donuts took a wrong turn." He picked up a mini-donut that had gotten stuck beneath a weight. "Boy, this thing is heavy, certainly heavier than any donut I've ever seen. I guess that explains how they're able to do so much damage."

"And by the looks of it, that thing is definitely not a donut," Velma added. She

That's one weird-looking donut.

looked at it closer. There was a tiny ring of small metal beads inside. "When was the last time you had a donut with ball bearings in it?"

"Rast reek?" Scooby asked.

"No, Scoob," I said, shaking my head. "Those weren't ball bearings. Those were chocolate sprinkles."

#6

Like, that was when things really got intense! Not only was Metal Man gone, now Daphne was, too. We really needed to find some clues to solve this case! Did you notice anything that might be a clue? Turn the page and get through the next puzzle as quickly as you can to find out for sure if we found anything clue-worthy.

Puzzle #6

Unscramble each of the clue words. They're all things you'd find in a gym.

Then, take the letters that appear in the ⬭ boxes and unscramble them for the final message.

RCKELO MORO

L O C K E R   R O O M

SANAU

S A U N A

LUDBEBLM

D U M B B E L L

YAOG TAM

Y O G A   M A T

CIRXESEE KIBE

e x e r c i s e   b i k e

GICMINBL WLLA

C L I M B I N G   W A L L

AND THE CLUE IS:

M I N I A T U R E   W H E E L

Like, man, you're doing great! The miniature wheel that Fred found was our second clue! With your help, we'll get to the bottom of this caper in no time at all. But there's still more detective work to be done, which means there's more chances for us to bump into that oversize baked good. Still interested in hanging around?

From the desk of
Mystery, Inc.

Fred and Velma hadn't found anything when they went to check the locker room and front desk computer.

I was about to tell them all about the really neat jump rope machine Scoob and I had found, but decided not to — like, I didn't want it to seem like Scoob and I were fooling around! That's something we would never do! 😊

"Our next step is to see where that mirrored door leads," Fred said.

"Do we have to?" I asked nervously.

"You and Scooby could stay out here and wait for the Devilish Donut to come back," Velma suggested.

"Ro ray!" Scooby barked.

The four of us crossed the gym to the long mirrored wall. As we got closer, we realized that the mirrors lining the walls were all doors!

"Jinkies, there must be — " Velma began, then stopped to count the doors. "At least twenty doors here."

"Well, there's only one thing to do," Fred

said. "Start opening. I'll start on this end. Velma, you start on the other. Shaggy and Scooby, start in the middle."

We all took our positions. I reached out, but there was no doorknob.

"Like, how do we open these things?" I asked. Fred pushed against the right side of the doors — it popped open with a click. I saw how it was done.

"C'mon, Scooby," I said, "let's get pushing!"

Scoob and I pressed against a mirrored

door, and it swung open a bit. I opened it all the way and called, "Anybody in here?"

We were in a small, dimly lit room. There was a pile of floor mats in the corner. Soothing music played through a speaker on the ceiling. Like, this was a room meant for napping if I've ever seen one! A door on the far wall of the room had a sign that read, "Locker Rooms."

"This yoga room has a back door to the locker rooms," Fred said.

"I guess I know our next stop," Velma said, and nodded.

"Velma, you and I should go back to the locker rooms through the gym," Fred suggested. "Shaggy, Scooby, you two follow the back hall. That way, we'll cover both entrances to the locker room."

Fred and Velma walked back through the gym, leaving me and Scooby alone in the yoga room.

"Well, we've got our marching orders, Scooby," I said. "May as well get it over with."

We passed through the rear door to the locker room. We found ourselves in a long, narrow corridor. The hall was carpeted and well lit, with pictures of flowers and mountains and waterfalls covering the walls.

"Man, it's awfully quiet in here, Scooby," I said.

"Reah, roo riet," Scooby agreed.

"Whaddaya say we pick up the pace a bit?" I asked. This place was giving me the creeps.

We began running down the hallway until we came to a huge cart piled high with dirty towels. The cart sat just outside the locker rooms.

"I guess we should wait here for Fred and Velma," I said. Then a terrible thought crossed my mind, and I had to share it with my best buddy.

"What if they never come out? Like, what if that donut demon got them already?" I asked. "Then we'd be the only ones here. All alone."

The tension was getting to be too much for us. We heard a muffled shout and jumped ten feet in the air.

"DONUT!" I screamed. We turned around and ran back down the hall. We raced through the yoga room and back out into the gym, where we ran smack into Fred and Velma.

"ZOINKS!" I cried.

"RUH-OH!" Scooby yelled.

"Take it easy, fellas," Velma said. "It's just us."

Once we calmed down, Fred explained that neither he nor Velma found anything in the locker rooms. Then Fred noticed something.

"Quick, Velma," Fred said, "take a picture with your camera!

Can you spot what Fred noticed? The answer to the puzzle on the next page will let you know if you're on the right track.

Puzzle #7

Place each word from the list below in the correct position. Be careful though, because one word may fit in more than one space. When you've filled in all the words correctly, the double-underlined letters will spell — from top to bottom — the last clue.

AEROBICS   HEALTH   YOGA
EXERCISE   WORKOUT   DUMBBELL
SWEAT   CRUNCHES   PULL UPS
CARDIO   MUSCLE

From the desk of
Mystery, Inc.

"This gym has got a lot of stuff in it that we can use to catch the monster, but it's going to take all of our help," Fred said. "So here's my idea."

Fred explained that Scoob and I should lure the mini-donuts into the yoga room and barricade the doors. While that was happening, Fred and Velma would go up to the running track and unfasten the cargo net.

"After that, Shaggy and Scooby, you lure the big donut monster into position beneath the track," Fred continued. "Then Velma and I will drop the net and capture it."

"Great plan, Fred," I said. "But I've got one question."

"What's that?" asked Fred.

"What if the monster shows up before we have a chance to get everything set?" I asked.

Fred and Velma stared at me in disbelief.

"Shaggy, in all the years we've been solving mysteries, we've never had that problem," Velma said.

"Well, there's a first time for everything!" I said. "Look!"

Fred and Velma spun around and saw the donut demon rolling toward them.

"Jinkies!" Velma exclaimed.

"Let's get moving!" Fred instructed. "Shaggy, Scooby, get the donut to chase you

Run, Scooby, run!

now! Velma and I are going up!"

Scooby-Doo and I ran around the gym with the giant donut monster in pursuit.

"Scooby, what are we supposed to do?" I asked.

"Roga room!" Scooby replied.

I nodded. "Right," I said. "Let's go!"

Scooby and I ran in and out of the different yoga rooms. Lines of mini-donuts rolled after us. Since we hadn't had time to make any kind of barricade, we had no way of locking the minis in the rooms.

"I've got an idea, Scooby!" I called. "Follow me!"

I ran across the gym to the area where the treadmills stood. I jumped onto a treadmill and turned it on. Just as the train of minis rolled onto the treadmill with me, I jumped off and sped up the controls. The mini-donuts got stuck rolling on the treadmill. Scooby-Doo saw what I had done and did the same thing. Soon all of the mini-donuts were caught rolling along on the treadmills.

"Way to go, pal!" I said, high-fiving my best bud.

"RAHAHAHAHA!" laughed the giant evil donut as it hopped directly toward me and Scoob. "Two for the price of one!"

"Over here!" Fred yelled from the track above, motioning at us.

"This way, Scooby-Doo!" I called. We started running toward Fred and Velma. But the donut creature sensed that something was up. It rolled in the opposite direction, making a large circle in order to come up behind us. Fred and Velma tried to reposition themselves on the upper track, but the cargo net was too heavy to move quickly.

"Let's go, Scoob!" I called, taking off across the gym. Scooby turned to run but tripped over an exercise ball. By the time he got up, the donut demon was right on his tail.

"Run, Scooby, run!" I cried. Scooby took off and ran all over, weaving in and out of the various pieces of exercise equipment. The donut maneuvered remarkably well for a baked good. Scooby-Doo ran between the posts of the automatic jump rope machine. His front paw stepped on the remote control that was lying on the ground. Just as the donut monster arrived, the rope began turning.

"WHHHHHOOOOOAAAA!" cried the donut, doing its best to bounce along in the rhythm of the jump rope. "Get me off of this thing! HELP!"

Fred and Velma now had plenty of time to move the cargo net. But before they could, the donut tripped itself up. The automatic jump rope sent the monster flying into the mirrored wall with a *WHOMP!* The donut dropped to the floor with a dull *THUD!*

Fred and Velma ran downstairs from the track and joined me and Scooby, where we were standing over the donut.

"Great job, Scooby!" Velma said.

"Great job, everyone!" Fred said.

"Sorry I couldn't be of more help," Daphne said, coming over to them. Metal Man was close behind. "But we were a little tied up."

"Yeah, that gargantuan piece of freaky fried dough tied us up and stuffed us into the dirty towel cart," Metal Man said.

"At one point, I heard Shaggy and Scooby's voices," Daphne said. "I tried to scream, but I guess they didn't hear me."

"Oh, so that muffled sound we heard in the hallway was really you?" I asked.

"How'd you get free?" asked Velma.

Daphne explained that she and Metal Man finally wriggled free and made it out in time to watch the donut monster slam against the mirrored wall.

Mystery, Inc.

gets their man . . .
er . . .

. . . baked good!

"Well, we're really glad to see you safe and sound," Fred said.

"Not as glad as we are to be out of that towel cart," Metal Man said. "Remind me to wash those towels more often!"

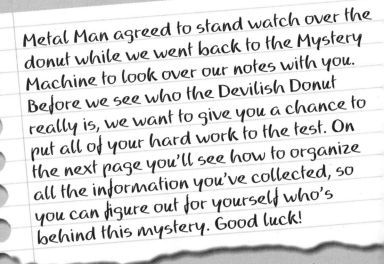

Metal Man agreed to stand watch over the donut while we went back to the Mystery Machine to look over our notes with you. Before we see who the Devilish Donut really is, we want to give you a chance to put all of your hard work to the test. On the next page you'll see how to organize all the information you've collected, so you can figure out for yourself who's behind this mystery. Good luck!

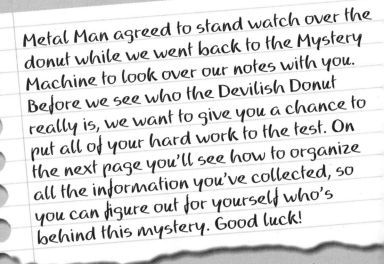

Shaggy's Entry #8

Solution

Take the solutions from each of the puzzles and write them in the chart below according to the instructions:

SUSPECTS Write the name of the suspect from each of the puzzles:	CLUES Write the clue from each of the puzzles:		
	Puzzle #5 Solution:	Puzzle #6 Solution:	Puzzle #7 Solution:
		X	X
Puzzle #2 Solution:		X	X
Puzzle #3 Solution:	X		
Puzzle #4 Solution:	X		

Put an X in the suspect's clue box if he or she can be connected to that clue.

When you're done, there should be only one suspect with an X in each of his or her clue boxes.

Write that person's name here:

_____

When you think you've solved the mystery of the Devilish Donut, turn the page to go back to Metal Man's Muscle Factory with us.

From the desk of
Mystery, Inc.

Metal Man McGillicuddy walked over to the donut monster and poked at the creature.

"Rubbery," he said. Metal Man grabbed it with both hands and grunted mightily as he tore the costume open. He reached inside and pulled out a very sweaty and skinny man.

"Jackson Viney," Metal Man spat.

"Just as we suspected," Fred said.

"Really?" asked Metal Man. "And why would you suspect him?"

"It all has to do with the clues," Daphne said. "Right after the donut first showed up, we found a piece of a nutrition bar. But it wasn't your run-of-the-mill nutrition bar. It was homemade, and exactly like the ones Polly Fiberfeld was giving out."

"Wouldn't that mean that Polly was a suspect?" asked Metal Man.

Velma agreed but explained that Polly had told them that she had also given a bar to Jackson Viney but no one else — except for me and Scooby. And since me and Scooby had eaten ours, wrapper and all, the bar could

It was
Jackson Viney!

only have been dropped by one of two people:
Polly or Jackson.

"Interestingly, Polly, Jackson and Gayle
all had reasons for wanting to get back at
you, Metal Man," Fred said. "Polly because
you wouldn't let her give out her bars.
Gayle because you took her picture off the
brochure. And Jackson Viney because he never
got the muscles he wanted. So their motives
and connections to the first clue made them
all suspects."

"But how'd you get to Jackson Viney?" asked Metal Man.

"That's where the second clue comes in," Velma said. "It was one of the destructive mini-donuts that turned out to be an ultra-heavy wheel. In fact, it was just like a wheel you'd find on a pair of in-line skates that were adapted for fitness purposes."

"Like the skates Gayle invented and Jackson was supposed to have used for his training," Metal Man said, beginning to put the pieces together. "So I suppose that eliminated Polly."

Fred, Daphne, and Velma nodded.

"Which brings us to our third clue," Fred said. He held out the piece of the brochure. Metal Man didn't need more than a passing glance to recognize it.

"But why couldn't this be traced back to Gayle also?" he asked. "She said she had all the old brochures with her picture in them."

Daphne stepped forward. "Even though I wasn't around when they found it, I can answer that one," she said. "True, Gayle has all of the old brochures, but she said she had them on display at home. I don't think someone who was so proud of their own

If you follow my program in just six weeks you can begin to notice a difference!

picture would treat it so roughly." ✳

"Not only that, Jackson Viney was upset about what he thought was your old guarantee," Fred continued. He flipped the brochure over and showed Metal Man the circled words that referred to "noticing a difference in six weeks."

"So you did all this just because you didn't bulk up?" Metal Man asked Jackson.

Jackson's mood darkened. "Do you have any idea what it's like being the skinniest one in the room? I came to you for muscles, and I got nothing! Nothing!" Jackson said. "I wanted to make you pay for getting my hopes up and then not delivering. But all I got out of it was a splitting headache and a ruined donut costume. And it's all thanks to those meddling kids and their plodding pooch."

Metal Man shook his head sadly. "Jackson, you only get out as much as you put in," he said. "If you had followed Gayle's program — no matter how crazy — I'll bet you would have seen results. But these things take time, and for some people, more time than for others. If you're serious about getting into shape, then you have to commit to it all the way. And if you want, I'll be your personal trainer. And no roller weights. It's up to you, Jackson."

"That was awfully nice of you, Metal Man," Daphne said. "Especially after all the damage Jackson Viney did."

Metal Man shrugged. "It's not the first time I've dealt with a frustrated client," he said. "Jackson just went a little overboard. Plus, I've got insurance. Now then, how can I thank you kids for all of your help? How about lifetime memberships to the Muscle Factory?"

"Wow! That's great, Metal Man!" Fred exclaimed.

"But totally unnecessary," Daphne said. "We were glad to help . . . at no charge."

"Well, thanks, but I still feel kind of bad that I wasn't able to give your friends more of a workout," he said. Looking over, he saw that Scooby and I were each drooped over an exercise bicycle in exhaustion.

"I'd say they got more exercise today trying to avoid exercise than they've had in a long, long time," Velma joked.

"Don't worry, fellas," Daphne said. "We won't bother you about your snack habits anymore."

Scooby and I suddenly perked up.

"Like, did someone say snack?" I asked.

"How about a donut?" asked Fred.

Scooby and I made a face.

"I never thought I'd say this, but I think I've seen enough donuts to last me awhile," I said.

"Ree roo," Scooby echoed.

"Then how about a Scooby snack?" asked Daphne. She tossed it into the air. Scooby leapt up from the bicycle and gobbled the snack before he hit the ground.

"Rummy!" he smiled, wagging his tail and licking his lips. "Scooby-Dooby-Doo!"

Congratulations . . . you did it! We think you've got what it takes to be an honorary member of Mystery, Inc! So be on the lookout for more Scooby-Doo Case Files! We'll be glad to have you come along and help solve another mystery with me, Shaggy, and with Fred, Daphne, Velma, and of course Scooby-Doo!

Shaggy's Entry #9

See you soon!

No part of this publication may be reproduced in whole or in part, or stored in a retrieval system, or transmitted in any form or by any means, electronic, mechanical, photocopying, recording, or otherwise, without written permission of the publisher. For information regarding permission, write to Scholastic Inc., Attention: Permissions Department, 557 Broadway, New York, NY 10012.

ISBN 13: 978-0-439-81418-8

ISBN 10: 0-439-81418-9

Copyright © 2007 Hanna-Barbera.

SCOOBY-DOO and all related characters and elements are trademarks of and © Hanna-Barbera.

Published by Scholastic Inc. All rights reserved.

SCHOLASTIC, LITTLE APPLE, and associated logos are trademarks and/or registered trademarks of Scholastic Inc.

Designed by Michael Massen

12 11 10 9 8 7 6 5 4 3 2 1   7 8 9 10 11/0

Special thanks to Duendes del Sur for cover and interior illustrations.

Printed in the U.S.A.

First printing, April 2007

SCOOBY-DOO!

Case Files #1

The Devilish Donut

Written by James Gelsey

WORLDWIDE PUBLISHING

A
LITTLE APPLE
PAPERBACK

SCHOLASTIC INC.

New York Toronto London Auckland Sydney
Mexico City New Delhi Hong Kong Buenos Aires